Thank You, Mack!

An Ivy and Mack story

T0364515

Written by Juliet Clare Bell
Illustrated by Gustavo Mazali

Collins

Who and what is in this story?

Listen and say

bird

Ivy

Mack

Croc

book

Download the audio at www.collins.co.uk/839773

cat

Mack says, "Are you ok, Ivy?"

Ivy says, "I can't find my book."

Mack says, "Is it *this* book?"

Ivy says, "No. It's the book about the cat and the bird. The book from Grandma."

Mack says, "Don't be sad, Ivy. We can find it!"

Mack says, "Is it under *here*?
No, it isn't."

Mack says, "Croc can help."

Mack says, "Croc can't find *your* book. Would you like *THIS* book?"

Mack says, "You're sad, Ivy.
Would you like ..."

"... Croc?"

Thank you, Mack!

Mack says, "Are you happy now?"

Ivy says, "No. I'm sorry, Mack. I want my book from Grandma."

Oh dear.

Mack says, "Let's go in the garden.
You like the garden."

Ivy says, "Yes! Let's sit under the tree."

Ivy says, "I like this tree. It's a great place to sit and read."

Mack says, "I can read to you."

Mack says, "Now can you read to *me*?"

Ivy says, "That's Ok. This is a good place for books."

Mack says, "It *IS* a good place for books! *VERY* good! *Look*!"

Ivy says, "My book! Thank you, Mack!"

Picture dictionary

Listen and repeat

garden

Grandma

happy

sad

tree

1 Look and order the story

2 Listen and say

Collins

Published by Collins
An imprint of HarperCollins*Publishers*
Westerhill Road
Bishopbriggs
Glasgow
G64 2QT

HarperCollins*Publishers*
1st Floor, Watermarque Building
Ringsend Road
Dublin 4
Ireland

William Collins' dream of knowledge for all began with the publication of his first book in 1819.

A self-educated mill worker, he not only enriched millions of lives, but also founded a flourishing publishing house. Today, staying true to this spirit, Collins books are packed with inspiration, innovation and practical expertise. They place you at the centre of a world of possibility and give you exactly what you need to explore it.

© HarperCollins*Publishers* Limited 2020

10 9 8 7 6 5 4 3 2

ISBN 978-0-00-839773-9

Collins® and COBUILD® are registered trademarks of HarperCollins*Publishers* Limited

www.collins.co.uk/elt

British Library Cataloguing in Publication Data

A catalogue record for this publication is available from the British Library.

Author: Juliet Clare Bell
Illustrator: Gustavo Mazali (Beehive)
Series editor: Rebecca Adlard
Publishing manager: Lisa Todd
Product managers: Jennifer Hall and Caroline Green
In-house editor: Alma Puts Keren
Project manager: Emily Hooton
Editor: Deborah Friedland
Proofreaders: Natalie Murray and Michael Lamb
Cover designer: Kevin Robbins
Typesetter: 2Hoots Publishing Services Ltd
Audio produced by id audio, London
Reading guide author: Julie Penn
Production controller: Rachel Weaver
Printed and bound by: GPS Group, Slovenia

Download the audio for this book and a reading guide for parents and teachers at www.collins.co.uk/839773